THIS MAGI BOOK BELONGS TO:

LEWIS DEIGHTON

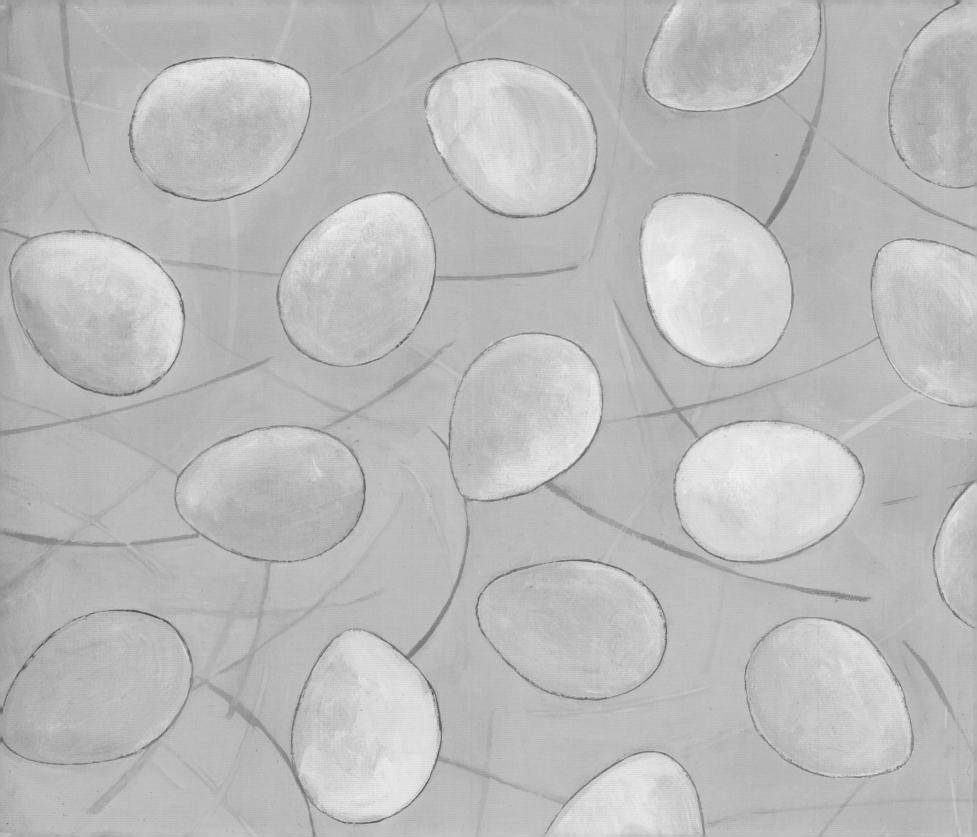

For Timothy and the
North Hampshire Hospital
Special Care Baby Unit
~J.S.

For Emily Anna
~J.C.

Reprinted 1998 (Twice)

This paperback edition published 1997

First published in 1997 by Magi Publications
22 Manchester Street, London W1M 5PG

Text © 1997 Julie Sykes
Illustrations © 1997 Jane Chapman

Julie Sykes and Jane Chapman have asserted their
rights to be identified as the author and illustrator
of this work under the Copyright, Designs and
Patents Act, 1988.

Printed in Belgium by Proost NV, Turnhout

ISBN 1 85430 407 0

DORA'S EGGS

by **Julie Sykes**

illustrated by **Jane Chapman**

Dora was sitting on a nest of eggs.
They were shiny brown and smooth
to touch.
"These are my very first eggs,"
clucked Dora proudly.
"I must get all my friends to
come and admire them."

Dora climbed out of the hen house
and into the farmyard.
"Who shall I visit first?" she asked.
"I know! I'll go and find Doffy Duck."

Dora hopped over the fence and across the field
until she reached the pond.
"Hello, Doffy," called Dora. "Would you like to
come and see my eggs?"
"I can't come now," quacked Doffy. "I'm teaching
my babies to swim."

Dora stood watching the ducklings
splashing around and learning to paddle.
Somehow she felt a bit less excited.
"My eggs are nice," she thought.
"But those fluffy ducklings are
much nicer."

Dora felt just a little sad as she trotted off to the
sty to visit Penny Pig.
"Hello, Penny," she clucked. "Would you like to
come and see my eggs?"
But Penny didn't hear. She was having too much fun,
tumbling around with her wriggly piglets.

Dora gave a little sigh.
"My eggs are nice," she said. "But those
wriggly piglets are much nicer."

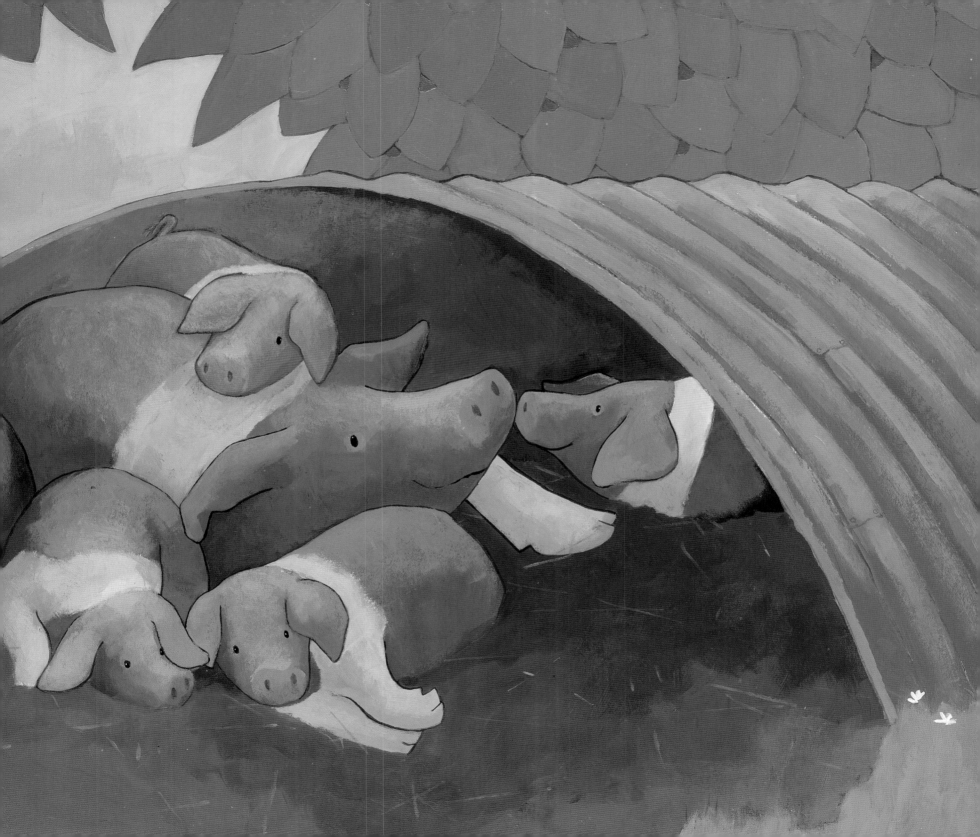

Dora gave another little sigh as she climbed the
hill to find Sally Sheep. "Would you like to come
and see my eggs?" she asked Sally.
"Not today," bleated Sally. "I'm too busy keeping
an eye on my lambs."

Dora looked at the lambs, frolicking in the field. She felt rather glum. "My eggs are nice," she thought. "But those playful lambs are much nicer."

Very sadly, Dora walked back to the farmyard.
On her way she bumped into Daisy Dog.
"Hello, Daisy," clucked Dora. "Would you like
to come and see my eggs?"
"Sorry, Dora," barked Daisy, wagging her tail.
"I can't come now. I'm taking my puppies
for a walk."

Dora was beginning to feel
quite miserable.
"My eggs are nice," she said.
"But those puppies out
for a walk are much nicer."

In the farmyard Dora stopped at the cowshed. She wished she felt happier, but perhaps Clarissa the Cow would cheer her up. "Would you like to see my eggs?" she called.

"Sssh," mooed Clarissa softly, nodding her head at the straw. Snuggled up by her feet and fast asleep was a newborn calf.

Dora felt like crying.

"My eggs are nice," she whispered. "But that little calf, all snuggled up, is much nicer."

Dora walked back across the yard in the
sunlight and climbed into the hen house.
Her eggs were just as she had left them,
smooth and brown and very still.
"My eggs are nice," sighed Dora, fluffing
out her feathers. "But everyone else's
babies are *much* nicer."

Very sadly, Dora settled
herself down on to
her nest . . .

CRACK!

Dora jumped up in surprise.

"Oh no!" cried Dora. "I've broken them!"
Tears began to roll down her face.
They splashed on to the nest and over
the cracked eggs. As each tear fell,
the cracks grew wider and wider until
suddenly . . .

. . . up popped a fluffy head,
then another, and another.

Soon the nest was full of tiny chicks.
"Cheep, cheep," the chicks squeaked.
"Cheep, cheep."
Dora stopped crying and stared.

It didn't matter that the eggs were broken.
The new chicks were everything
Dora had ever wanted!
Proudly she strutted out into the farmyard,
and one by one the chicks followed after her.
All the animals stopped and stared.

"Why, Dora!" quacked Doffy.
"They're as fluffy as my ducklings!"
"And wriggly like my piglets,"
oinked Penny.
"They're as playful as my lambs,"
baaed Sally.
"And you can take them for walks –
just like my puppies," barked Daisy.
"But best of all," mooed Clarissa,
"your chicks can snuggle up to you,
like my calf snuggles up to me."
"Cluck," said Dora happily, agreeing
with her friends. "My eggs were nice,
but my chicks are much, much nicer!"

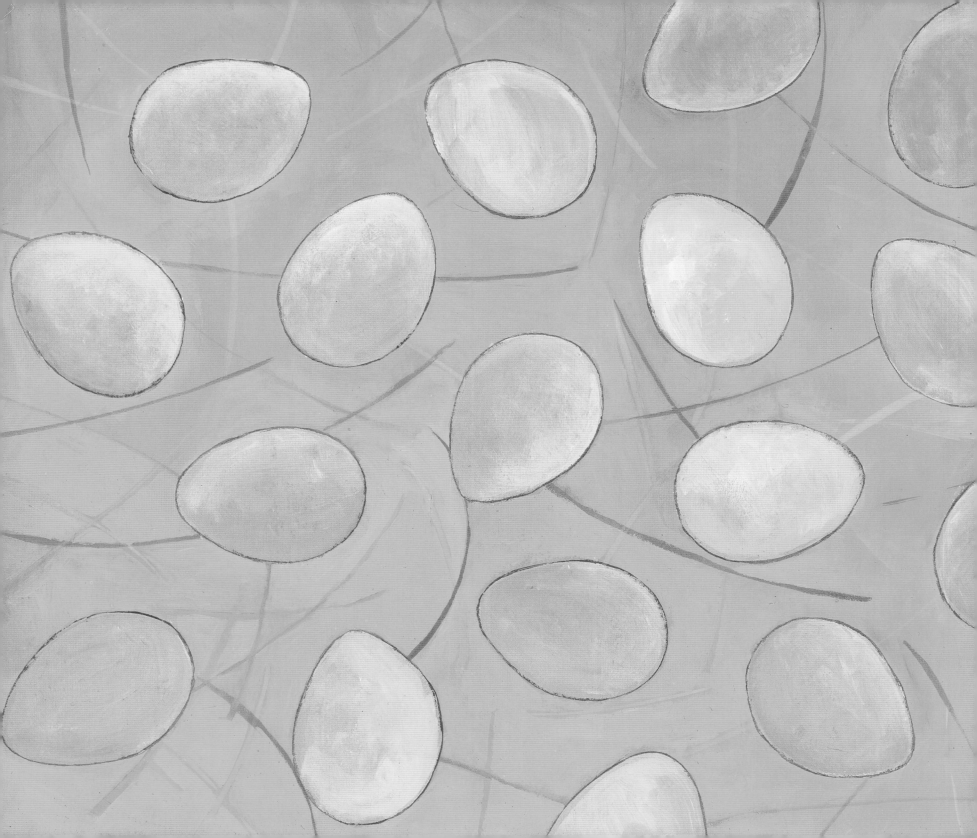

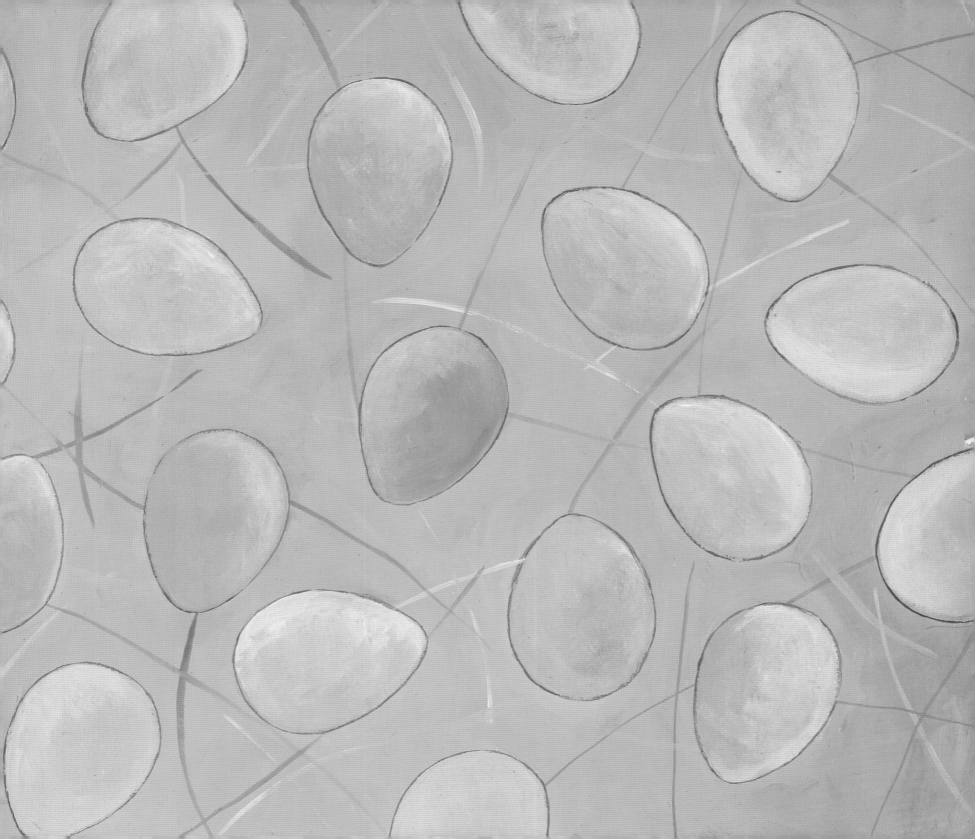

Some more books from
Magi Publications
for you to enjoy.

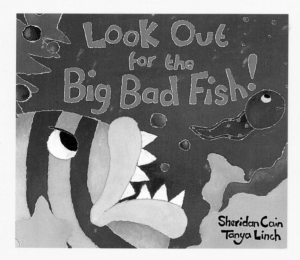

Look Out for the Big Bad Fish!
Sheridan Cain
Tanya Linch

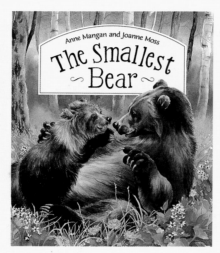

Anne Mangan and Joanne Moss
The Smallest Bear

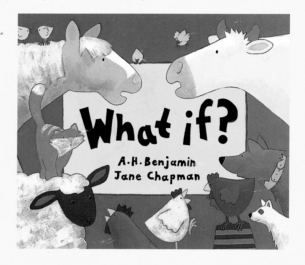

What if?
A.H. Benjamin
Jane Chapman

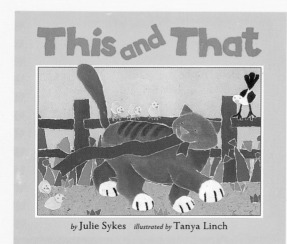

This and That
by Julie Sykes illustrated by Tanya Linch

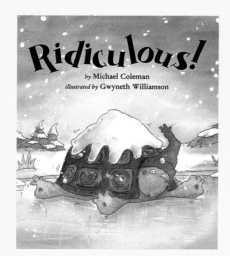

Ridiculous!
by Michael Coleman
illustrated by Gwyneth Williamson

I don't want to go to bed!
Julie Sykes
Tim Warnes

All books available from most booksellers. In case of difficulty please contact
Magi Publications, 22 Manchester Street, London W1M 5PG, UK